P9-CRP-373

TRAPPER

Written by: Stephen Cosgrove
Illustrated by: Robin James

PRICE STERN SLOAN
Los Angeles

Copyright © 1978 by Price Stern Sloan, Inc.
Published by Price Stern Sloan, Inc.
360 North La Cienega Boulevard, Los Angeles, California 90048
Printed in the United States of America. All rights reserved. No part of this publication may be reproduced, stored in a retrieval system or transmitted, in any form or by any means, electronic, mechanical, photocopying, recording or otherwise, without the prior written permission of the publishers.
ISBN 0-8431-0587-9

Serendipity™ and The Pink Dragon are trademarks of Price Stern Sloan, Inc.

20 19 18 17 16 15 14 13 12

Dedicated to the harp seals of Canada.
May they live in happiness
on a mythical island called Samrakan.

Stephen E. Cosgrove

In the crystal reaches of the stormy Atlantic Ocean, off the north coast of Canada, there was a small, frozen island called Samrakan.

The clouds floated freely there, dancing softly in the snow-filled sky as the ocean washed over the icy rocks.

Because of the crisp, brisk weather, furry little creatures called minstrel seals came from all over to play in the cold waters of the island. They were called minstrel seals because they always sang pretty songs to the sea.

The seals spent all of their days eating the delicious fish that lived deep in the bays, and sitting on the rocks and softly humming in the bright sunlight.

Every day, when the sun reached its highest, one of the seals would climb high onto the rocks and begin to sing a gentle melody to the sea. One by one, the other seals would join in harmony, until the most beautiful song was carried by the breeze for miles around.

They would sing like that for hours and hours, until a small minstrel seal called Trapper would join them and quietly begin to hum along. He would get so carried away by the pretty music that he would suddenly bellow out a sour note. It was so sour and so loud that the birds would lose their feathers in fright.

The other seals would cringe at the sound and, one by one, they would slide noisily back to the sea, leaving Trapper all alone on the island of Samrakan, humming all by himself, way out of tune.

It would have been the very same to this day except that the seals, one by one, started disappearing. Day by day, one or two seals would disappear and the group would be that much smaller.

The other seals didn't really mind because each one enjoyed his own pretty voice anyway, and with fewer seals they could hear themselves better. Besides, it seemed to Trapper that the fewer seals there were, the longer he got to sing along.

Finally, Trapper realized that there were only three seals, including himself, left on the whole island.

"Hmmm," he thought as he munched on his lunch in the bay. "This is getting stranger and stranger. I wonder where everyone has gone. My singing isn't very good but it can't be so bad that everyone would leave."

He decided that right after the singing next day he would watch carefully to see where everyone went.

The day dawned cold and bright. As he did every day, Trapper played in the surf, and when the sun was at its highest, he went to join the other seals.

He hummed along with the other two for the longest time until, as always, he sang out with a very sour note. The other two seals, with a "tsk" or two, began sliding back into the sea.

Trapper waited for just a moment, then slipped over to the edge of the rocks and looked below. There was the ugliest creature he had ever seen, and in his arms he had the last two seals on the island of Samrakan.

Trapper quickly hid as the creature ran off with his fellow seals. "That was close!" he thought. "But now I'll be able to sing pretty songs for as long as I like, with no one to say I'm singing wrong." He played in the bay and munched his lunch; everything almost stayed the same.

When the sun got to its highest point, Trapper again climbed the rocks to sing a song to the sea. He sang and sang, but it just wasn't the same. For what good is a pretty song if there's no one around to hear it? Trapper finally realized that he was all alone.

"What will I do?" he cried. "I'm afraid of the ugly creature, but without the other seals I have nothing."

He began swimming around the island, looking in all the bays for his friends, but to no avail. He climbed high onto the rocks and looked and looked. He searched throughout the day and long into the night, but never found a trace of the other seals.

Finally, he became so tired from his search that he climbed out of the water, found a soft patch of frosty grass, and fell fast asleep.

While he slept, he dreamed of all the days he had spent with the other seals and the pretty music they had shared.

Trapper was so tired that he slept the whole night through. He probably would have slept through the day had he not been shaken awake to find himself hanging upside down.

"What's going on?" he said with a yawn. Then he realized with a start that he was hanging in the arms of the creature.

"Aha! So, you're awake, my little singing minstrel seal. Soon you shall join your friends and you can all sing pretty songs for me."

"Who are you, and what do you want with me?" Trapper cried.

"My name is Muttsok, and I like pretty things. You are going to be part of my collection," he laughed. And with Trapper stuffed neatly under his arm, he headed away from the bay.

Poor Trapper did not know what to do. He thought and thought but was too scared to think of anything.

"I've got to calm down so I can think," he thought. Well, the only thing that would calm him down was to sing, so he began to hum softly to himself, so softly in fact that the creature didn't even hear. Then, as the song built within him, he bellowed his loudest, sourest note ever! The creature was so shocked by the terrible noise that he dropped Trapper so he could hold his hands over his ears.

Trapper hit the ground with a thud and quickly rolled into the safety of the sea.

Trapper hid beneath the waves, but when he realized the creature wasn't following him, he bobbed to the surface and looked around. There on the beach before him was Muttsok, stomping his feet and raging. "Come back here you dumb little seal! You're pretty and I want you."

"Muttsok," shouted Trapper, "why do you have to own everything that is pretty? Can't you enjoy a pretty thing the way it is?"

"No, you stupid seal. What's the fun of seeing something pretty if you can't take it with you?"

"Well," said Trapper carefully, "you can see a pretty sunset and you can't take that with you."

"I tried to take it once," growled Muttsok.

"Yes, but if you had succeeded, then no one else would have been able to see the sunset. Just like all the seals you took, now no one can hear their beautiful song to the sea."

"Well," grumbled the creature as he stirred his foot in the snow, "I still like to collect pretty things."

Trapper thought for a moment. "That's easy, Muttsok. I'll show you all sorts of pretty things to collect."

Trapper swam just a little way up the beach and shouted to Muttsok, who had followed. "Look! At your feet there are thousands of beautiful rocks. And look! Above you there are hundreds of pretty winter flowers growing."

Muttsok looked around and saw that there really were pretty things everywhere. He began picking up rocks; then he suddenly stopped. "If I take all the pretty rocks and flowers, then nobody can enjoy them either."

"Ahhh," said Trapper, "you take only the prettiest one and leave the rest for others to share."

So Muttsok took the prettiest rock. Then he climbed way up and picked the prettiest flower, and with them safely clutched in his hand, he rushed back to set the seals free.

After a while, things returned to normal on the island of Samrakan, and the minstrel seals once again sang their beautiful songs to the sea.

Some of the time Muttsok sat with a flower in his hand and a gentle smile upon his face, with small, silent Trapper by his side. If you listened very carefully, you could hear the two of them singing softly, out of tune.

IF YOU SEE THOSE PRETTY THINGS
THAT NATURE LIKES TO SHOW
REMEMBER ALL THOSE SEALS THAT SING
AND LEAVE THEM THERE TO GROW.

Written by Stephen Cosgrove
Illustrated by Robin James

Enjoy all the delightful books in the Serendipity Series:

BANGALEE	LEO THE LOP TAIL THREE
BUTTERMILK	LITTLE MOUSE ON THE PRAIRIE
BUTTERMILK BEAR	MAUI-MAUI
CATUNDRA	MEMILY
CRABBY GABBY	MING LING
CREOLE	MINIKIN
CRICKLE-CRACK	MISTY MORGAN
DRAGOLIN	MORGAN AND ME
THE DREAM TREE	MORGAN AND YEW
FANNY	MORGAN MINE
FEATHER FIN	MORGAN MORNING
FLUTTERBY	THE MUFFIN MUNCHER
FLUTTERBY FLY	MUMKIN
FRAZZLE	NITTER PITTER
GABBY	PERSNICKITY
GLITTERBY BABY	PISH POSH
THE GNOME FROM NOME	POPPYSEED
GRAMPA-LOP	RAZ-MA-TAZ
THE GRUMPLING	RHUBARB
HUCKLEBUG	SASSAFRAS
JALOPY	SERENDIPITY
JINGLE BEAR	SNIFFLES
KARTUSCH	SQUABBLES
KIYOMI	SQUEAKERS
LADY ROSE	TICKLE'S TALE
LEO THE LOP	TRAPPER
LEO THE LOP TAIL TWO	WHEEDLE ON THE NEEDLE
ZIPPITY ZOOM	

The above books, and many others, can be bought wherever books are sold, or may be ordered directly from the publisher.

PRICE STERN SLOAN
360 North La Cienega Boulevard, Los Angeles, California 90048